ole's Star

For my mother
B.T.

ORCHARD BOOKS

First published in Great Britain in 2018 by The Watts Publishing Group
First published in paperback in 2019

1 3 5 7 9 10 8 6 4 2

Text and illustrations © Britta Teckentrup, 2018

A CIP catalogue record for this book is available from the British Library.

HB ISBN 978 1 40834 282 4
PB ISBN 978 1 40834 283 1

Printed and bound in China

Orchard Books
An imprint of Hachette Children's Group
Part of The Watts Publishing Group Limited
Carmelite House, 50 Victoria Embankment, London EC4Y 0DZ

An Hachette UK Company
www.hachette.co.uk
www.hachettechildrens.co.uk

BRITTA TECKENTRUP

Mole's Star

Mole lived deep under
the ground. He loved his
cosy home of burrows, dens
and tunnels. But sometimes he
felt a little lonely in the dark.

Every night, Mole popped his head out of his molehill
to say hello to the stars. He sat on his favourite rock,
gazing at the beautiful twinkling lights in the sky.

One night, as Mole sat on his rock, he saw a dazzling
shooting star, and quickly closed his eyes to make a wish.

"I wish I could own all the stars
in the world," he whispered.

When Mole opened his eyes,
he couldn't believe what he saw.
There were ladders all around him,
leading up into the sky.

Mole didn't think
twice. He scurried up and
down the ladders, collecting the
stars one by one, and carrying
them home.

That night, his burrow was
full of shimmering starlight.

Mole loved his
bright new home
so much, he
wanted to stay
there for ever.

But as the days
went by, he started
to miss his favourite
rock. So one evening,
he popped his head
out of his molehill,
and saw . . .

. . . nothing.

The sky was dark.

Deer stood in the clearing with tears in her eyes.
"Where are all the stars?" she said.

Field Mouse shook his head sadly.
"My children love to stargaze while I sing
their bedtime lullaby. They will be so sad."

"The stars help me find
my way," said Fox.
"Where can they be?"
sighed Bear.
"I have flown far
and high," said Owl.
"The stars are gone."

Mole felt terrible. He didn't know the other
animals loved the stars as much as he did.
He scurried into the trees, hiding himself away.

Mole walked deeper and deeper into
the forest. What had he done?

Then Mole saw something glinting through
the trees. A star lay in a puddle, its light faded and
dull. Could it be his special shooting star?

Mole bent close. "Oh, how I wish I had never
taken the stars," he whispered.

The star began to twinkle . . .

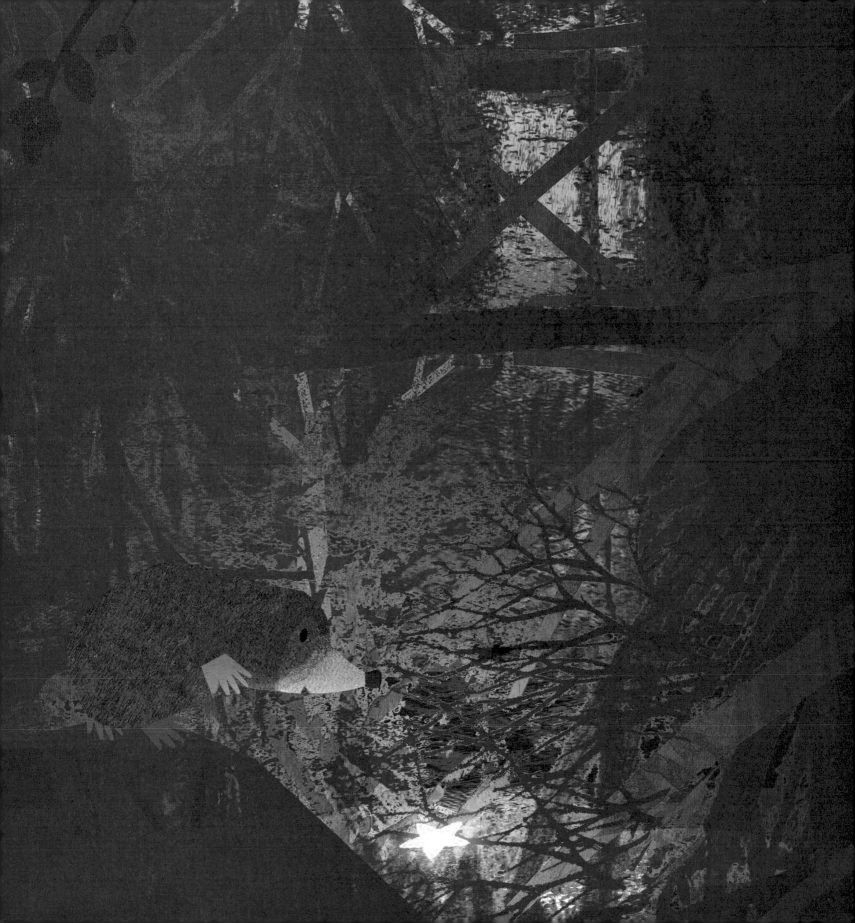

. . . and ladders appeared.

Mole didn't think twice. He rushed back
to the clearing, the star lighting his way.
"I'm sorry," he cried. "I took the stars. I wanted
them for myself, but now I know the stars
belong to everyone. I'm going to
put them back."

"I will help you," said Deer.
"We will help too," said
Field Mouse, Bear, Fox and Owl.

The animals worked
all through the night.
One by one,
they put each
star back where
it belonged.

Last of all, Mole placed his special star above his
favourite rock. From that night on, it shone
brighter than ever. And all the animals in the
forest could share the wondrous light
of the twinkling night sky.